CASE
3

The Case of the
CREEPY
CONVERTIBLE

Library of Congress Cataloging-in-Publication Data
Manley, Michael, 1953–
The case of the creepy convertible/by Michael Manley.
p. cm. —(A Clooz Calahan mystery; case #3)
Summary: Clooz Calahan is stunned when a beautiful client describes why she
believes her 1962 Corvette convertible is haunted. [1. Robbers and outlaws—
Fiction. 2. Automobiles—Fiction. 3. Ghosts—Fiction. 4. Mystery and detective
stories.] I. Title. II. Series: Manley, Michael, 1953– Clooz Calahan mystery;
case #3.
PZ7.M31289Car 1999   96-27932
[Fic]–dc20

Text copyright ©1999 by Michael Manley

Illustration copyright ©1999 by Sanford Kossin

Cover and book design by Robin Benjamin

Silver Burdett Press
A Division of Simon & Schuster
299 Jefferson Road, P.O. Box 480
Parsippany, NJ 07054-0480

For further information about <u>Ranger Rick,</u>
write to: <u>Ranger Rick</u> Magazine
          8925 Leesburg Pike
          Vienna, VA 22184
or call at: 1-800-588-1650

ISBN 0-382-39687-1 (LSB) 10 9 8 7 6 5 4 3 2 1

CASE
3

The Case of the
CREEPY
CONVERTIBLE

BY MICHAEL MANLEY

Silver Burdett Press
Parsippany, New Jersey

The brand-new alarm went off and scared us out of our wits. The last thing we were expecting was a visitor on this lazy Saturday afternoon. Before Clooz could do anything, a blond head popped through the trapdoor in the bottom of our treehouse crime lab.

"Mary Beth!" Clooz shouted. "I told you not to come to the lab anymore without an invitation. . . ."

His voice trailed off as a beautiful blond head came into full view. It wasn't the blond head he was expecting, and for one of the few times since I've known him, Clooz Calahan was speechless.

"Are you Clooz Calahan, the detective?" the blue-eyed beauty asked softly.

Clooz's one brown eye and one blue eye sparkled in silent admiration.

She said, "Cat got your tongue?"

Well, Clooz could make a fool of himself in front of a pretty girl, but not me. "It's him," I croaked.

She turned those big eyes on me and asked my name. Somehow I had forgotten it.

"Matthews," Clooz answered. "His name is Matthews. He's my assistant."

She shook my hand. Hers was cool and dry. Mine was wet and sticky, and after we shook, I sensed her wanting to wipe hers on the leg of her shorts. But she was too classy for that.

"I'm Amanda Van Buren," she said.

"Dr. Van Buren's daughter?" I asked.

She nodded.

Clooz finally got his act together and stuck out his hand. "Clooz Calahan," he said, handing her his card.

She read it and smiled a bright white smile. "So you're the detective. I didn't expect you to be so cute."

Oh boy, you could have lit a match on Clooz's face. In fact, he kind of looked like a match—a bright red face, with a shock of light-red hair on top. I'd never seen him smile like that.

He reached out and retrieved the card (it was the only one he had). "Nice to meet you, Amanda," he said, his face returning to normal. "What can we help you with?"

She sighed and sat down on the edge of a ragged

recliner. "Well, it's my car. It's really cool, a '62 Corvette that my grandfather bought for my mom on her sixteenth birthday. On my sixteenth birthday, my mom gave it to me."

"That *is* cool." I said. "How could that be a problem?"

Clooz shot me a look that told me to shut up and listen. He's always telling me I should talk less and listen more. Says I'd learn more that way.

"Well," Amanda continued, "lately I haven't been able to drive it."

"How come?" I asked, again getting the shut-up look from Clooz.

"It's kind of silly."

"Amanda," Clooz said, "there are no silly cases."

She smiled a thank-you, then turned very serious, and blurted out, "I'm pretty sure my car is haunted."

Chapter 2

"**H**aunted!" I said. "How can a '62 Corvette be haunted?"

"I . . . I was kinda hoping Clooz could find out for me, but I guess it's stupid. That's why I couldn't go to the police. Maybe I'd better just leave."

She made a move for the trapdoor, and Clooz moved smoothly between her and the exit.

"It's not stupid at all, Amanda. Matthews and I would be happy to take your case."

Speak for yourself, Romeo, I thought. Ghosts and stuff were not my cup of tea.

"Right, Matthews?"

I smiled my best smile and said an enthusiastic "Yes!" Oh, dopey me.

About that time our alarm went off again. This

time the blond head that Clooz had originally been expecting (I probably should say dreading) popped through.

"Mary Beth, I told you that the treehouse is off limits to girls!"

Mary Beth coolly walked in and perched on the edge of Clooz's desk.

"Oh, yeah?" She pointed to Amanda. "Then what's that?"

"Amanda's no girl, she's a client," I said.

They all looked at me as if I'd lost my marbles. Maybe I had. But, as usual, Clooz came to my rescue.

"What Matthews means is that Amanda is here on business, not just to be a pest like some females we know."

"Yeah, yeah, yeah, Calahan," Mary Beth said. "You know you can't live without me." She stuck out her hand to Amanda. "Mary Beth Wainwright," she said.

"Amanda Van Buren."

As I watched them shake hands, I was amazed at how much the girls looked alike, from the color of their hair and eyes, down to the almost identical shoes they were wearing.

"Are you a detective, too?" Amanda asked Mary Beth.

"Well, I have helped on a few cases," she replied.

"No, she's not part of Clooz Calahan Investigations," Clooz said, giving a dirty look to Mary Beth.

In truth, Mary Beth really *has* helped us solve some of our toughest cases. Her dad is Judge Wainwright, and her access to police records through the judge's computer has helped us bring several criminals to justice. She's a royal pain sometimes, but the truth is she's smart, determined, and in spite of what Clooz says, I think she's necessary to the team. I also think she's a little sweet on Clooz, but she'd never admit it.

My name is Matthews, and I'm Clooz's right-hand man. Clooz is definitely the brains of the outfit, but I kind of provide the muscle. I'm no tough guy or anything, but I guess I'm handy to have around when the chips are down.

Some people wonder why I want to hang around with a scrawny, carrot-headed kid detective like Clooz Calahan, but the fact is, we're a team. And being a member of a winning team is just about the best feeling you can have.

"So, what's your problem?" Mary Beth asked Amanda.

"My car's haunted."

"Mary Beth!" Clooz warned.

Mary Beth ignored him as usual.

"Cool," she said. "Let's check it out."

Clooz rolled his eyes and, knowing he'd lost the first round, led the way out of the treehouse.

Amanda lived in a nice neighborhood with trees lining the streets and gardens full of flowers. It was a quiet, peaceful neighborhood. The only person I saw was a teenager leaning against a tree across the street.

We walked up a long driveway that curved toward a big house that looked like it should have been on a peaceful lake instead of in the middle of town.

Amanda reached into her purse and brought out her car keys. She pressed a button on a small gadget attached to her key chain, and the garage door began to crawl upward. There in the garage sat an awesome red-and-white Corvette.

The car was beautiful, and I watched as Clooz gently ran his hand over the smooth fiberglass fenders. "A '62 in mint condition. It's a beauty."

"Thanks," Amanda said. "I just wish I felt better driving it."

"Why do you think it's haunted?" Mary Beth asked.

"Well, sometimes I'm just standing here in the garage, and the engine starts all by itself. Other times, the windows will roll down by themselves, or the doors will lock or unlock."

"Weird," I said.

"Yeah, it's pretty scary."

And, as if on cue, the engine suddenly started.

Chapter 3

We all took a quick step backward. The Corvette just sat there and purred. Then, the driver's window slowly lowered, then raised. The door locks popped up and down.

Clooz walked over and crawled into the driver's seat. There were no keys in the ignition. As he sat there, the engine died. He shook his head and got out and closed the door.

"Very strange," he said, the freckles on his cheeks bouncing up and down.

"No joke, Sherlock," Mary Beth said. "The question is, what are we going to do about it?"

"Well, Mary Beth, I'd like to say *we* aren't going to do anything, that Matthews and I will handle it, but I guess there's no use. Somehow you always wind up involved anyway, so I guess you might as well be in on the case from the beginning. So, what do you suggest?"

This took her by surprise, and she didn't know what to say. One of the few times I've witnessed that particular event.

"That's what I thought," Clooz said, and turned to Amanda. "I assume by your having a control on your key chain, you have an alarm on the car?"

She nodded. "It's the first thing I did when Mom gave me the car. Why?"

Clooz ignored the question. He was in charge now, and he was asking the questions.

"Who installed the alarm?"

"A kid by the name of Johnny Starke. He works for Mr. Chavez at his garage and installs car stereos and alarms in his spare time."

"I think we'll pay Mr. Starke a visit," Clooz said.

Jose Chavez's garage sat on a corner in the older part of town, which was now being rebuilt. In the spirit of the refurbishing, Chavez had built a new garage whose design fit in with all the other buildings being constructed in the neighborhood. It was a modern facility, with the latest in computer technology to tell him what was wrong with the cars he was trying to repair.

Behind the new shop was the building where Chavez

had started in the business. It was still in reasonably good condition, but it was old and not very modern. This was where Johnny Starke installed car alarms and stereos. It was also the headquarters of the 6C's—the Constantly Cool Car Club of Calhoun County. Starke lived in a small room in the back.

We walked into the new shop. There were several cars lined up with the hoods raised, and mechanics in greasy coveralls bent over the engines, with only the bottom parts of their bodies visible, as if they were being swallowed by huge steel beasts. A young man with coal-black hair looked up from the hood of the car closest to the entrance and walked over.

"Hey, Clooz, good to see ya," he said, giving Clooz one of those complicated handshakes that seem to take five minutes.

"This is Tony Chavez, guys," Clooz said. "His dad owns the shop." He introduced each of us to Tony.

"What's up?" Tony asked.

"Amanda here has a problem with her car. It's doing some weird things. Johnny installed her alarm, so we thought he might know what was wrong with it."

"That's cool. Johnny is taking a break out back. You guys go on out there and see him. I'll be there as soon as I finish up this job."

As we headed toward the back door of the shop, Mary Beth said, "Cute guy."

Amanda agreed. Clooz just rolled his eyes.

"I don't know," I said. "He looked just like a normal guy to me."

"Are you kidding, Matthews? That guy was a hunk. Didn't you see that black hair and those beautiful brown eyes?" Mary Beth said.

"Well, I didn't really notice."

Mary Beth looked at Amanda. "He was really checking you out."

Amanda blushed and smiled. "I think I may have car trouble more often."

Mary Beth cracked up, and then Clooz cleared his throat.

"Mary Beth, do you think you could keep your mind on the case? It's not very professional to get personally involved with the suspects in a case."

"Suspect? There's no way Tony could have anything to do with Amanda's car."

Clooz looked at Amanda. "As Mary Beth should know, everyone is a suspect until the investigation rules them out."

Mary Beth stuck out her tongue at the back of Clooz's head.

"I saw that, Mary Beth," Clooz said, pointing to their reflection in the back window of the shop.

We went through the back door of the shop, which led to the older shop. The difference was astounding. Where the new shop was spotless and modern, this one was dirty and old. Cobwebs stretched from the ceiling and dust covered most of the surfaces. A '57 Chevy was strewn on the shop floor in a million pieces.

"There's Johnny," Amanda said, pointing to a sulking figure sitting at an old workbench. The kid's face was like a piece of chiseled rock, his chin sharp and his jaw square. Blond hair hung to his shoulders in wiry strings, covering one of his dull green eyes.

"Johnny," Amanda called.

He raised his head to see who had called, then went right back to his work without acknowledging our presence.

We approached him and he continued to ignore us. "Johnny, I'm Clooz Calahan," Clooz said, and held out his hand.

Nothing from Johnny.

I thought this was kind of rude and reached over and touched his arm. Johnny shot off his stool, scattering his work over the bench. I hadn't realized how short he was—no taller than Mary Beth.

"Don't ever touch me, man!" he yelled, glaring up into my eyes with no fear.

We all jumped back in amazement.

"Hey, I was just trying to get your attention," I said, hoping not to rile him again.

Johnny stared a hole in me.

"Johnny, these guys want to ask you some questions about my car. It's acting funny; the windows are rolling down and the engine is . . ."

"What do you need these brats for? Are you so stupid you can't ask your own questions?"

Amanda looked as though he'd slapped her.

I thought this guy was a candidate for the Jerk of the Year Award.

Clooz decided to try again. "Amanda has retained us to investigate the unusual behavior of her car. Since you installed the alarm, we thought you might be able to help."

Johnny's bottle-green eyes bored through Clooz's skull. "You thought wrong, detective boy. Now take your little kiddie friends and get out. I don't know nothing about your windows rolling and your engine starting or anything else. Now get out! Girls aren't even allowed in the club."

He plopped back down on his stool and ignored us.

"You don't have to act like a jerk," Mary Beth said, taking a step toward him. "You can't keep girls out of here or anywhere else. I'll have my dad bring you up on charges of discrimination."

Johnny stood up, acting really angry. "I don't care what you do, as long as you get out of here and leave me alone."

Mary Beth started to move closer to him, but I stepped between them. "Let's go, Mary Beth, we can finish this argument another day."

She jabbed a finger at Starke. "And you can count on *that*."

Chapter 4

As we stepped out of the old shop, Tony was just coming out of the new one.

"Find out what you needed?" he asked, addressing Amanda.

"Johnny told us what we needed to know," Clooz said quickly.

We all gave him a puzzled look and, of course, Mary Beth started to say something, but I jabbed her in the ribs. Amanda wisely sensed she should stay quiet also.

"Great," Tony smiled, still looking at Amanda. "The rest of the club will be voting on your membership application soon."

"Excellent," Amanda said. "I'll keep my fingers crossed."

Tony gave her a wink. "I'll put in a good word for you. Gotta go now," he said, and rushed off.

"I thought girls weren't allowed in the club," Mary Beth said.

"They're not usually," Amanda answered. "But since I'm a car nut and I have a really cool car, they might make an exception."

"If it's up to Tony they will," Mary Beth said.

"Yeah, but if it's up to Johnny, you don't have a prayer," I said.

We walked back toward Amanda's house, and Mary Beth asked Clooz, "Why did you tell Tony that Johnny told us everything we needed to know?"

"Because Johnny mentioned that Amanda's engine started, but she never said that. He cut her off before she could tell him."

"And there's something else," I said. "When we were at Amanda's house before, I noticed someone leaning against a tree across the street. I'm pretty sure it was Johnny."

"Looks like Johnny has some explaining to do," Amanda said.

"Fat chance that jerk will tell us anything," Mary Beth said. "I'd like to catch that guy with some incriminating evidence. I'd bust him good."

Clooz smiled. "Funny you should say that, Mary Beth, because I think you may just get your chance."

That night found us crouched behind a bent-up, rusted-out '55 Ford. We were behind the Chavez's old shop, among a bunch of junked-out cars, waiting for Johnny to leave for the evening. Amanda wasn't involved with this stakeout, even though she'd wanted to come. Clooz won't allow clients along on stakeouts, especially with someone as nutty as Johnny Starke.

This stakeout was a long shot because Johnny lived right there in the shop. We were hoping he'd go out for the evening and we could look for evidence, in particular a remote control that matched Amanda's.

The shop was enclosed with a chain-link fence, and I wondered why anyone would fence in a garage. I was enlightened when a door opened in the back of the shop and out rushed two rather large dogs, black-and-tan ones. I think they're called Rottweilers. It only took the dogs a few seconds to catch our scent, and they came running right toward us, barking their heads off.

"Quick, on top of the car!" Clooz hissed, and the three of us scurried on top of the old Ford.

"Clooz, someone will hear!" Mary Beth said.

I was thinking it might be better to be discovered than to become some mutt's dinner.

"Follow me!" Clooz said, and he started jumping from the top of one car to the other.

Mary Beth didn't need to be told twice and took off after him. As usual, I was bringing up the rear. We were doing pretty well until one of the dogs figured out how to get on top of the cars, too.

"Clooz! One of them is up here!" I shrieked.

"Just run, Matthews!"

That was easier said than done. It was clear I wasn't going to set any speed records as I sprinted from the top of one old car to another.

The dog was right on my heels, and I could smell his breath behind me. His partner was on the ground trotting alongside us, ignoring the other two morsels ahead and concentrating on the sure meal—me.

I heard Mary Beth say, "Oh, no" and then disappear from sight. The answer to her disappearance was a mystery even I could solve; she'd run out of cars to run across and was on the ground out in the open. Clooz was there, too. And so was the dog.

I could see the door of the garage. It was either that or get eaten.

"Clooz, head for the door!"

He ran for it, tugging Mary Beth along with him. The dog was almost there and I was too, but I didn't have anywhere to go. There was a dog in front of me and a dog behind me. I could see that Clooz and

Mary Beth had made it, but I could also see that I wouldn't be joining them.

Suddenly a light flicked on and a voice yelled, "Jake, Mack! Heel!"

Magically, the dogs stopped their barking and froze, both of them now staring at me.

Johnny Starke stepped out the back door and smiled at me. "Why don't you join your friends inside where it's safe?"

He let out a laugh that sent chills up my spine.

Chapter 5

Johnny had company. There were three other guys, each as scruffy as Starke, with greasy hair and tattoos. They were all grinning an evil grin. Maybe it was contagious.

"Glad you could drop in, kids," he said. His friends snickered. None of us said anything.

Starke walked up to Clooz. "Want to tell me what you were doing out back?"

When Clooz remained silent, Starke grabbed his collar and twisted. Clooz's face turned red, but he didn't say anything.

"Hey, leave him alone," I said, muscling my way between Starke and Clooz. I guess Starke was feeling taller with his friends there. They stood up and took a step toward us, but I couldn't back down now.

"Sticking up for your little friend, kid?" Starke asked with a smirk.

"I'll do what I can," I said, sounding a lot calmer than I felt.

Starke stepped back but kept up his threats. "I think me and the guys here can handle whatever you come up with."

The friends agreed.

"Now, I'm going to ask you again, what were you doing out back?"

This time Clooz spoke up. "We were waiting to see if Tony came to the clubhouse tonight. We wanted to talk to him."

"Oh, yeah? What about?"

That stumped Clooz for a minute.

"I wanted to see if I could join the club, too," Mary Beth spoke up.

Our buddy Starke got a big laugh out of that one. "You're kidding. You don't even have a car."

"So? I still like them," she said defiantly.

"You can forget that, little girl. No girl is ever going to be a member of the 6C's."

"What about Amanda?"

Mary Beth just couldn't leave it alone.

"She doesn't have a chance either," he said.

While this pleasant little conversation had been going on, I noticed Clooz was searching the room with his eyes. They came to rest on Johnny's desk, and I moved slightly to where I could see better. Ah, so that was what he was fixed on! A remote transmitter just like the one Amanda had. The only problem was getting it. What we needed was a distraction.

We got it when Mary Beth called Starke a jerk.

"Hey there, smart mouth! You need to watch what you say."

"Frankly, I agree with her," I said. "Someone who thinks Amanda would even consider going out with a punk like you has got to be a jerk."

He reached out and grabbed me by the shirt. "I don't have to take anything from you, sonny boy."

Man, the things I do to solve a case!

I grabbed his shirt right back. He looked surprised when I did that and relaxed for just a second. I shoved with all my strength and sent him flying right into his friends. They all landed on the floor in a pile. "Let's get out of here!" I yelled, and ran for the door. Clooz and Mary Beth were right behind me. Because of the dogs, we couldn't go out the back like we'd come, so we headed out the front.

The only problem was that the only place to go was into the new shop. That would have been okay, except the door was locked. We were trapped.

Starke and his friends stepped out the door and slowly approached us. After all, there was no hurry.

Johnny snapped his fingers, and each of his pals took hold of one of us.

I struggled against the guy's grip, but he was too strong. I decided to fight him with words.

"The dog's breath smelled better than yours."

That got him. Silenced by the tongue of the assistant investigator.

"Okay, boys and girls, my friends here are going to show you what happens to little kids who mess with us," Starke said. "Show 'em guys!"

Right then the shop door burst open and there stood Tony.

Chapter 6

"**W**hat's going on here?" Tony demanded.

Starke's friends looked to him for an answer.

Knowing the pressure was on, Johnny spoke up. "Caught these kids snooping around out back. I was just trying to find out why."

"He was trying to break our necks," Mary Beth clarified.

Tony frowned. "Anyone hurt?"

We all shook our heads.

"Okay, then. Starke, if I ever hear of something like this again, you're out of here. Now you and your friends get out of my sight."

Starke started to argue, but the look on Tony's face stopped him dead. He and his buddies sulked off.

"Thanks, Tony," Mary Beth said.

"No problem. If he bothers you guys again, just let me know. Johnny's not such a bad guy when he's not with his friends. I guess he has to show off around them."

We nodded in understanding.

"I was wondering," Tony said, "what *were* you guys doing behind the shop?"

Clooz looked a little uncomfortable, and I figured he was making something up. To my surprise, he told the truth—pretty much.

"Tony, I'll be honest with you. We were spying on Johnny. I'd rather not say any more right now, because I'm not sure and I don't want to falsely accuse anyone. But I promise I'll tell you the whole story as soon as we solve the case. Fair enough?"

Tony thought about it for a second and agreed. "I can live with that," he said.

"Great. Well, we'd better be going."

We waved and headed down the brightly lit street.

"That was pretty slick what you told Tony," I said.

"Nothing but the truth," Clooz replied.

"I hope this is not the beginning of a trend," Mary Beth said.

We all laughed.

"Where to now?" I asked.

"I think we'll walk by Amanda's house and try out this transmitter." He grinned, holding it up.

I'd forgotten all about it. "You got it!"

"What's that?" Mary Beth asked.

"It's a transmitter I found in Starke's apartment. I'm betting it matches Amanda's."

We wowed Amanda with the story of our adventures that night.

"Wish I could have been there," she said.

"It's just as well you weren't," Clooz said. "Johnny seems to really resent you."

"You're probably right," she said. She led the way to the garage. "Let's go see if Starke is as big a creep as we think."

We walked out into the darkened garage, and Amanda pressed the button on the wall that raised the garage door. A bright light came on at the same time.

Clooz walked to the car and held up the transmitter. "Ready?"

We all nodded eagerly.

Clooz pressed the button on the right and the engine roared to life. Another press of the button and the windows began rolling down.

"Yeah! You solved the case!" Amanda squealed. "My car's not haunted!"

"Well, aren't you the smart bunch of little detectives," a voice behind us said, and Johnny Starke walked out of the darkness and into the garage.

Chapter 7

"**J**ohnny, what are you doing here?" Amanda demanded.

"Oh, I just thought I'd follow the kids here and see what they were up to," he smirked. "Couldn't help but notice the transmitter was gone, and I put two and two together."

"We're smarter than you thought we were, eh?" Mary Beth said.

Starke grunted and removed the hood of the dark-blue Dallas Cowboys sweatshirt he was wearing. "Oh, yeah, real little Sherlocks. But let me tell you this, kiddos, if I ever catch you snooping around my place again, your buddy Tony won't be able to save your hides."

"Oooh, I'm scared," Mary Beth answered.

"Mary Beth!" I warned. Her mouth was going to get us in trouble—again.

Amanda spoke up. "What I don't understand is why you did this to my car, Johnny."

His face softened a little. "I guess I thought you'd be impressed and want to go out with me."

"That's got to be the joke of the year!" Mary Beth said.

Johnny's face reddened, and he took a step toward Mary Beth. "I've heard about enough of your smart mouth, little girl."

"Johnny! That's enough!" Amanda said. "What you did to me was mean and cruel. You had me scared to drive my own car. I don't see how you thought that would make me want to go out with you."

Johnny had softened up again, and his face was flaming. He shrugged and shook his head.

"Johnny, I want you to leave and I don't want you to ever speak to me again!" Amanda said.

"Fine, if that's the way you want it, little rich girl. But I want you to remember you'll pay for this."

"I don't think so, Johnny. I've already paid; it's your turn next."

"That's right. You're the one that's going to pay, you creep," Mary Beth said. "If it's the last thing I do, I'll see that you pay."

Johnny snorted and walked away without saying another word.

Clooz had been quiet through all the talk, but now he spoke up. "Mary Beth, you shouldn't challenge Johnny like that. He could really do something terrible."

"I hope he tries," she replied.

"Why have you got it in for Johnny so bad?" I asked. "Amanda is the one that he played the trick on."

"I just can't stand to see someone treat a girl like that. Men have been treating women like that for centuries and I'm sick of it. He doesn't want Amanda in the car club, but he sure wants to take her out. I hate it when boys act like girls aren't equal. It really gets me riled up. And that jerk is gonna pay."

No one said anything for a minute and then Amanda spoke up. "I really appreciate you guys solving the mystery of my haunted car. I can't wait to start driving it again!"

With that, she bent down and gave Clooz a big kiss on the cheek. His face exploded into a flare of crimson.

Chapter 8

The kiss was good news (for Clooz). The bad news was that Amanda asked us if we'd keep an eye on her house for the next few nights. She was afraid Johnny would do something nasty after our little run-in.

Just like most men who are impressed with a pretty girl, Clooz agreed—for both of us.

So, there we were, squatting behind some bushes, swatting at bugs that were making us their dinner, and waiting for Johnny to hatch his next plot against Amanda. Conveniently, Mary Beth said she had other plans and couldn't accompany us. Anyway, I figured since we were onto him, Starke wouldn't dare try anything. I mentioned that to Clooz.

"Maybe that's what he wants us to think, Matthews. But I've got to admit it seems unlikely."

Boy, was I ever wrong! Just before midnight I glimpsed movement across the street. I tugged on Clooz's sleeve and pointed.

A figure in a hooded sweatshirt was making his way toward Amanda's garage. A second later the door moved upward, and we heard the engine of the Corvette start up even before the door reached the top of its journey. In the light we could tell only two things about the intruder—he had on a hooded Dallas Cowboys sweatshirt and was wearing white Aero sneakers.

He slipped into the car and backed down the drive.

"Quick! The bikes!" Clooz said.

We grabbed them and pedaled for the driveway.

"Try to block him in!" Clooz yelled.

Yeah, right, I thought to myself, but nonetheless pedaled like crazy straight for the driveway entrance.

The thief saw us and gunned the car. It shot backward and would have run over Clooz if he hadn't swerved at the last second. The driver screeched to a halt in the street and threw the car in gear. The tires of the car squealed as he sped down the street.

We pulled our bikes around in pursuit, but the Corvette was way too fast for us. It turned right on the highway and headed out of town.

Clooz and I ground to a stop at the intersection and sat there a minute catching our breath.

"See his face?" Clooz asked.

I shook my head. "You?"

"Uh-uh, but I did see a strand of blond hair flying out of the hood."

"Johnny?"

"Must have been, but I can't say for sure."

"So what now?" I asked.

"I guess we go tell Amanda someone stole her car."

And that's what we tried to do, but no one answered the doorbell or our knocks. Puzzled, we called it a night.

Clooz and I were in the lab the next morning, trying to figure out what to do about Amanda's car, when the phone rang. Clooz hit the button on the speaker phone, and Amanda's voice came over the wires.

"Clooz! You guys get over here quick. My car's been stolen!"

"Yes, we know," Clooz said calmly.

"You do?"

"You did ask us to watch your house last night."

"Oh, yeah. So you saw Johnny steal it?"

"We saw *someone* steal it," Clooz said.

"Well, why didn't you stop the thief?" she asked.

"We tried, but he or she attempted to run us over."

"Oh, I'm sorry, Clooz. I don't know what I was thinking. Did you call the police?"

"Not yet. We wanted to talk to you first and search the area for clues. We tried to tell you last night, but no one answered your door."

"Uh, well, my parents were out of town."

"I figured you'd answer the door yourself."

"Well, uh, I was spending the night with a friend."

It was my turn to speak up. "You mean, you had us stake out your house and risk getting killed, and you were off at a slumber party?"

Clooz frowned at me but didn't say anything.

"Well, you know, it was, uh, a last minute thing."

"Right," I said with a huff in my voice.

There were a few minutes of silence and she finally said, "Uh, you guys coming over?"

"Sure," Clooz said, and hit the button to disconnect the call.

Neither of us were happy campers.

She was standing in the driveway when we got there.

"Have you called the cops yet?" Clooz asked.

She shook her head, saying nothing, knowing she was not number one with us right then.

"Good. We'll check the area for clues and then give Detective Merkin a call."

Clooz asked her to stand beside the driveway, and we began to search the area in a grid pattern. When we got to the area just in front of where the car had stood, Clooz bent down and nudged something from under a workbench with his pencil.

"What is it, Clooz?" I asked.

"It appears to be a ballpoint pen." He rolled it some more to reveal the writing on the pen.

"What's it say?"

"Chavez Auto Repair."

"That proves Johnny stole my car!" Amanda said.

Clooz shook his head. "It only proves that someone dropped a pen here that has an ad for Chavez Auto Repair. I bet hundreds of people have these pens. Mr. Chavez probably gives them to all his customers."

She looked disappointed. "I still think Johnny stole my car."

"That's possible, but we'll have to prove it before he can be arrested," Clooz said.

He took a sandwich bag from his pocket and scooted the pen into it, careful not to touch it.

"What're you going to do with it?" I asked.

He thought about it a minute. "I'm going to take it back to the lab and check it for fingerprints."

"Oh, boy. Won't that make Detective Merkin mad? And what if Detective Sergeant Steele takes the call? He'll kill us for sure!" I said.

Sergeant Steele is a cop who really hates our role in some of the cases we've solved. He's always telling us to stay out of police business or he'll put us in jail, but he hasn't yet. He's come close a couple of times, though.

"I'll turn over any findings I discover in my examination of the evidence. This has been our case from the start and I want us to solve it. The only reason I want to call the police at all is for Amanda's insurance. She'll need a police report for the insurance company."

I had a bad feeling about this, but hey, he's the boss. I just didn't know how bad this was going to be.

Chapter 9

Oh, man, was Sergeant Steele glad to see us. And boy, was he angry! The only way it would have been worse was if Mary Beth had been there.

Clooz had called Detective Merkin, who is sometimes sympathetic to our investigating. Unfortunately, it was his day off, and Clooz had no choice but to talk to Sergeant Steele.

"Wait right there, you little creeps," I heard Steele's voice boom from the earpiece of the phone. Sometimes I think that guy doesn't need a phone. He can yell loud enough to be heard without one.

Anyway, he pulled up in his plain white Chevy and stomped up to the garage. There was an unlit cigar clenched in his teeth, and his face looked like a flaming bulldog. He was hot in more ways than one.

"Calahan, do you *make* crimes happen around you?"

"No, sir," Clooz said respectfully.

Steele looked at him kind of funny, then regained his meanness. "Okay, what's the story?"

Clooz filled him in on everything that had happened so far, from Amanda telling us about her car being haunted to finding out about Johnny Starke setting up the car to appear to be haunted.

"Sounds like I need to have a talk with young Mr. Starke," Steele said.

"That would be where I'd start," Clooz said.

"Yeah, well little Mr. Sherlock, you just keep your freckled nose out of this case. I'm tired of you always sticking it where it doesn't belong. At least the judge's daughter isn't mixed up in this one."

As if on cue, Mary Beth stepped into the garage.

"What's up, guys?" she asked innocently.

Steele turned redder and moaned.

"I was just telling your little friend here to stay out of this investigation, and since you're here, I'll tell you too—stay away. Got it?"

We all nodded our heads and he stared at us one by one, as if to read our minds to see if we were telling him the truth. Finally, he turned and stomped back to his car, got in, and drove off.

"Boy, that was really perfect timing," I said. "Steele was just saying that at least *you* weren't in on the case, and *poof,* here you are. You psychic or something?"

She laughed. "Nah, I just happened to be in the neighborhood and thought I'd stop by to visit Amanda."

Clooz had been shuffling his feet impatiently for a few minutes. I could tell he was eager to get back to the lab and check the fingerprints on the pen.

"Well, we'd better be going," I said, and Clooz looked grateful.

Clooz and I headed back to the treehouse crime lab.

"I was afraid Mary Beth would want to come with us," he said.

"Yeah, me too. She seems to have made friends with Amanda, though."

He nodded. "They seem to have a lot in common. Have you noticed how much they look alike?"

"Uh-huh. They could almost be sisters. They even dress alike."

We climbed into the treehouse and I watched while Clooz checked the fingerprints on the pen. First, he took it out of the bag, using a large pair of tweezers, and laid it on the workbench. Next, he dusted it with black fingerprint powder, then gently brushed the powder off with this real soft brush. Then, he applied a special tape to the pen and pulled it off. On the tape a fingerprint magically appeared.

He repeated the process until he had lifted all the

prints from the pen. He then stuck them under the microscope and looked at them. Finally, he took a set of prints out of his file, compared them to the ones lifted, and frowned.

"What is it?" I asked. "Did the prints match some in your file?"

He nodded. "There are two prints on the pen. One I suppose is Starke's, though I'll have to get a sample of his sometime soon. The other set, unfortunately, matched prints I already have on file."

The suspense was killing me. Clooz always drags out an answer, just to build suspense. He knows it really burns me up. I had to ask.

"Well, whose is it?"

He turned those multicolored eyes on me, and almost whispered. "The prints belong to Mary Beth."

Chapter 10

"**T**he prints belong to Mary Beth? Clooz, are you absolutely sure?"

He nodded solemnly and motioned me over to the microscope.

"See these swirls here?"

"Yeah?"

"Now look at these."

He was right—they were identical.

"But how can that be?"

"Well, there's one obvious explanation."

"Uh-uh. No way Mary Beth stole that car."

"*We* know that, but put yourself in Sergeant Steele's position." Clooz stuck one finger in the air. "One. She doesn't like Starke very much. That's a motive to frame him." Clooz stuck another finger in the air. "Two. She has access to Amanda's house. That's opportunity."

"Yeah, but that could be a coincidence."

"True. But it could also be a coincidence if those are Johnny's prints on the pen, too. He could claim it fell out of his pocket when he was working on the car or something. He's got an excuse. But as far as I can tell, there's no reason Mary Beth's prints should be on a pen found at the crime scene."

He had a point. It didn't look good for us.

About that time the alarm went off, and seconds later a blond head popped through the trapdoor.

"Hi, guys. What's happening?" Mary Beth asked.

Clooz hurriedly shoved the pen and stuff into a drawer before she saw them. He looked as guilty as a cat that just swallowed its master's pet hamster.

"Uh, nothing, just hanging out," I said.

She stared at me and asked, "You okay, Matthews?"

"Fine, fine," I said, hoping I sounded more convincing to her than I did to myself.

I guess she bought it because she changed the subject.

"Pretty bad about Amanda's car, huh?"

Clooz and I nodded like those dogs with the springy necks that sit in the back windows of cars.

"I bet Johnny Starke stole it, don't you?"

"Well, Mary Beth, a good investigator never jumps to conclusions. There might have been others with a motive to steal the car, too." Clooz said.

She thought about that a minute, then agreed. "Yeah, I would have liked to have stolen it and framed old Johnny with it, but since he probably stole it anyway . . ."

"Mary Beth, you shouldn't say things like that. People might get the wrong idea," I said.

"Whatever," she said. "Everybody knows Johnny stole the car, so what's the difference?"

"We should let the police decide who to accuse, Mary Beth." Clooz said.

She tossed her blond curls. "Whatever."

The alarm went off again and another head popped through the trapdoor. "Hi, guys," Tony Chavez said as he pulled himself into the treehouse.

"Hi, Tony," Mary Beth said sweetly.

Oh, pulleeese. I thought I might throw up.

"What's up, Tony?" Clooz asked.

"I think I may need your help. One of the guys in the club just found an abandoned car out by Hunter's Pond and towed it in. I thought you could find out if it's stolen or anything. I mean, we'd like to keep it. It'd make a great project car."

"What kind of car is it?" I asked.

"Don't tell me," Clooz said. "It's a '62 Corvette, right?"

Mary Beth's eyes grew wide. "Amanda's car!"

Chapter 11

We hopped in Tony's car and rode over to the 6C's clubhouse, stopping on the way to pick up Amanda. She was thrilled that her car had possibly been found.

"Don't get too excited, Amanda," Tony said. "After you see it, you might not want it, even if it *is* your car."

We pulled up in front of Tony's dad's shop.

"It's around back in the clubhouse," Tony said.

We walked in and saw the Corvette squatting on the concrete floor, tires flat, mud and moss dripping from the bottoms of the doors.

"Yuck!" Mary Beth said.

"My car!" Amanda moaned.

"Are you sure it's yours?" Tony asked.

Amanda nodded. "You were right. I hate to admit it, but it's mine."

"Darn!" Tony said. "I thought for sure we'd found the next club project."

"We may not have a club to do projects if you keep letting girls in the clubhouse," Johnny said, stepping through the door from his room.

"You're just mad 'cause you didn't hide Amanda's car well enough when you stole it!" Mary Beth said.

"Hey, you little brat, I didn't steal nothin'!"

"Yeah, right," she said. "Maybe they can teach you proper grammar while you're rotting in prison."

Johnny lunged at Mary Beth and Tony barely managed to get between them. "Okay you two, that's enough! We'll let the police sort out who did what."

Clooz emerged from the office and announced that Sergeant Steele would be there shortly.

"You'll be in trouble then, you creep," Mary Beth mumbled.

"Mary Beth, that's enough," Clooz said.

She quieted down and walked over to Amanda, who was just standing there looking at her car.

"Who would do such a thing?" Mary Beth said, more to herself than to anyone.

"It stinks, all right," I said.

We all stood around and looked at the car until we heard the screech of tires outside. Sergeant Steele appeared a few seconds later.

His face was its customary crimson and the ever-present unlit cigar was in his mouth.

"Anyone touch it?" he demanded.

"Just the guys who found it in the pond and hauled it in," Tony said.

"I'll need them to go to the station house and get their fingerprints taken." He turned to Clooz. "Figured you'd be mixed up in this. You're sure you or your little friends didn't touch it?"

"Sergeant Steele, I'm well aware of the procedures of a criminal investigation. As Tony explained, no one has spoiled the crime scene."

Steele glowered at us, but let it go at that. In a few

minutes a tow truck appeared and whisked away the stolen car.

"When can I get my car back?" Amanda asked Sergeant Steele.

"We'll have to hold it for a while as evidence. You'll be notified when it's released."

We were walking back to the lab when Amanda asked, "You guys really think Johnny stole my car?"

Before anyone could answer, Mary Beth spoke up. "You can take it to the bank. Johnny figures if you don't have a car, you can't get in the club. The only thing he didn't plan on was someone finding the car."

"Clooz?" Amanda asked. "What do you think?"

He thought for a moment before he spoke. "Johnny certainly had a motive, along with the opportunity. He could have easily stolen the car, using an extra transmitter. But as an investigator, you have to be careful of the obvious and wait until all the evidence is in before you come to a conclusion."

"I've got all the evidence *I* need," Mary Beth said.

"That's why I would like you to stay away from the investigation," Clooz said.

Mary Beth stopped dead in her tracks. "You what? I've been on this case from the beginning. You can't just take me off now."

"Mary Beth, you've done the very thing a good investigator can never allow to happen."

"Yeah, what's that?"

"You've lost your objectivity."

"You don't have to be objective if the answer is staring you right in the face, Clooz."

Clooz just shook his head.

"Fine. If that's the way you want it, then I won't come around anymore." She turned to Amanda. "Come on, let's get away from these guys. Looks like all men are the same." The girls walked away as we stood on the sidewalk and watched.

"Do you think that was necessary, Clooz?" I asked.

"I'm afraid so, Matthews. Whether we like it or not, Mary Beth is a suspect in the case. We can't allow her to be involved until we prove she's innocent."

"I guess you're right, but it seems a little harsh."

The phone was ringing when we got back to the crime lab. Clooz hit the button on the speaker phone and Detective Merkin's voice came from the box.

"Thought you'd want to know, we just picked up Johnny Starke for the theft of Amanda Van Buren's car."

"That was fast," Clooz said.

"We lifted Starke's prints from the interior. Given everything else that's happened, that was all we needed."

"Thanks for letting us know, Detective Merkin." Clooz thought of something else. "Detective, were there any other fingerprints in the car?"

"Only one set besides the kids who recovered the car and Amanda's."

"You know whose they are?"

"Not yet. Why?"

"Uh, just wondering."

"Come on, you never just wonder about anything."

Clooz thought it over for a minute. "I'll make you a deal, Detective Merkin. If you'll fax over the set of prints, I'll check them out, and if I find anything, I'll let you know."

There was silence on the line, then, "Okay, but don't let anyone know I did this."

"Sergeant Steele will never know."

Clooz hit the off button and sat there quietly.

"You think those fingerprints might be Mary Beth's don't you?"

Clooz shrugged. "Maybe."

His fax machine rang and paper started to inch out. "We'll know in just a minute," he said.

Clooz snatched the paper out of the machine and pulled out his magnifying glass. Then he laid the two sets of prints side by side. He didn't need the magnifying glass. Even I could tell they were a match. The fingerprints belonged to Mary Beth!

Chapter 12

Clooz and I met at the treehouse early the next morning.

"What'll we do now, Clooz?"

"Beats me, Matthews. My first thought is to work on the case, but I'm afraid of what we might find if we solve it."

"But we have to know the truth, don't we? I mean, we can't let Johnny go to jail if he's innocent."

"You're right," he answered, and fell into deep thought. He looked like a worried little kid instead of a master detective, sitting there in his faded blue jeans, worn Aeros, and T-shirt with the picture of an eye and the word *private* printed over it.

The alarm went off and Tony popped up through the floor.

"Hey guys, guess you heard about Johnny."

We nodded.

"I don't think he did it."

We started to argue, but he held up his hand.

"I know he comes across as kind of tough, even mean sometimes, but he's had a really rough life. Now he's finally got the opportunity to make something of himself, and I don't think he would blow it."

"What about the thing with haunting Amanda's car?" I asked.

Tony shook his head sadly. "An error in judgment. He thought Amanda would be impressed with his cleverness. I mean, he really likes her, and he doesn't know how to show it."

"That's the understatement of the year," I said.

"Maybe so, but that doesn't make him a car thief."

"True," Clooz said, "but he did threaten Amanda."

"He was embarrassed. He didn't know how else to defend himself."

We all thought about that for a minute.

"So what do you want us to do?" Clooz asked.

"I want you to find out who really stole Amanda's car," Tony answered.

"It could turn out that Johnny really did it," warned Clooz.

"I'm willing to take that chance," Tony said solemnly.

"Okay, we'll do it, but we'll need your help."

Uh oh. This didn't sound so good. It could turn out that Mary Beth did it, and we'd be obligated to tell. Like Tony said, a chance we'd have to take.

"Sure," Tony said. "Where do we start?"

"First thing, I'd like to examine the place where the car was found," Clooz said.

"Sure."

"Have the cops been out there?" I asked.

Tony shook his head. "I don't think so. They nabbed Johnny so fast, I'm not sure they've looked any further."

"Good," Clooz said, grabbing his crime-scene kit. "Lead the way."

We pulled up to the lake in Tony's car just in time to run into Sergeant Steele. Boy, was this our lucky day.

"What are you kids doing here?" he demanded.

"Just thought we'd spend a little time with nature," Clooz said, smiling. "You know, listen to the birds sing, watch the squirrels play . . . "

"Search for clues," Steele finished.

"I'm tellin' you, Calahan, you better keep your nose out of this case." He held up his thumb and finger showing a gap too small for a gnat to fly through. "I'm about this close to running you in for interfering."

Clooz shot him his most innocent look. "I'm sorry, Sergeant, but I don't know what you mean."

"*Hummph,*" Steele grunted. "You know exactly what I mean, kid, and you better listen for a change."

"Find anything interesting?" Clooz asked, changing the subject.

"None of your beeswax," Steele said childishly.

"Okay, well, we'll just look around if you don't mind. I don't see any crime scene tape around anywhere."

"Go ahead, Calahan. The longer you fool around out here in the woods, the less chance you'll have to screw up the investigation somewhere else." He got in his car and sped off.

"Boy, that guy really doesn't like you," Tony said.

"It's because Clooz solved some cases the cops couldn't," I said proudly.

"Cool."

Clooz was all business. "Let's begin the search by using a grid pattern. Either of you see anything, don't touch it. Give me a yell, and I'll collect the evidence."

"The car was in the pond just down that hill," Tony said.

We headed down the hill, then started off in different directions per Clooz's instructions. I hadn't gone far when I noticed a small footprint in the mud real close to where the car was discovered. There were a lot of other footprints around, but they were all of large men's shoes, probably the cops'. That small one caught my attention; it looked familiar.

"Clooz, over here," I called.

He stuck a small stick in the ground to mark where he stopped searching and carefully made his way to where I was standing.

I pointed to the soft ground where the tiny footprint was pressed into the mud.

"Looks like a girl's shoe," Clooz said.

"Yeah, that's what I thought, too."

"Unlikely a cop would have a shoe that small," he said.

"Funny-looking sole. I think I've seen a sole like that before."

"Me too," he said.

"Where?"

"Where do you think?"

"Mary Beth has shoes like that!"

He nodded. "So does Amanda. Remember when we were talking about how they looked and dressed alike?"

I snapped my fingers. "That's right. We said they were like sisters."

I thought about that while Clooz got out his stuff to make a cast impression of the footprint.

"You think they have the same size foot?" I asked.

"Dunno," he said. "Not if we're lucky. Amanda's taller and older, but Mary Beth has kinda big feet. We'll have to check it out."

"How?"

"We'll cross that bridge when we come to it."

Tony wandered over to where we were working.

"Came up dry," he said.

"We may have something. A small footprint, like a girl's," I said.

"What's he doing?"

"He's making an impression of the footprint so that we can study it more closely in the lab. By pouring plaster of Paris into the footprint and letting it dry, we can get a copy of the print."

"Cool."

Clooz stood up and brushed himself off. "Let's finish our search while this is drying." He wandered off toward the stick he had stuck in the ground, and Tony and I continued searching my grid.

A few minutes later we heard Clooz give a yell. "Got something!"

We trudged through the underbrush in his direction and found him staring up into a tree. Tony and I couldn't see a thing. I was afraid that maybe the sun was getting to him.

"Whatcha looking at, Clooz?" I asked.

"Hair."

I squinted and moved closer.

"Watch your step!" he cautioned. "There's another footprint."

I looked down and sure enough a print that looked just like the other we'd found was at my feet.

I still hadn't seen the hair Clooz was looking at, though. He was grabbing the air with a pair of tweezers. He couldn't quite reach high enough to grab it. He looked at me like, Well, aren't you going to help?

I cupped my hands in front of me, and he stepped in them with one foot.

"Got it!" he said proudly.

As he brought what he had grabbed down to eye level, I could see it was a long blond strand.

"Looks like Amanda's hair," Tony said.

Clooz and I silently gave each other a look. We were both thinking the same thing—it's like Mary Beth's hair, too.

Chapter 13

We returned to the treehouse toting two plaster casts and a strand of hair. It was better than nothing, but the best part was that the cops had missed the evidence. Tony had to go back to work, so it was just Clooz and me.

"I realize we've got some potential evidence here, but how do we check it out? I mean, we can't very well just ask for a strand of hair and a footprint from Mary Beth and Amanda, can we?"

"You've got a point, Matthews," Clooz said. "We'll have to keep our eyes open for an opportunity. The first thing we should do is compare the casts to make sure they came from the same shoe."

"They look the same to me," I said, wondering why we were wasting our time. As usual, Clooz was able to show why he's the detective and I'm just the assistant.

He held his magnifying glass over the impression of each shoe in turn. He kept saying "hmmmm" and "uh-huh" to himself, but not letting me in on anything. Finally, I couldn't take any more.

"Okay, Clooz, I give up. What do you see?"

"You tell me," he said, handing me the glass.

I held it over the impressions of the soles of the shoes. They looked just like the soles of shoes to me— ugly shoes at that.

"See it?" he asked, the excitement building.

I knew he'd seen something. I looked harder.

Then I saw it.

"The word AERO on one is complete, but on the other, the E has three horizontal marks missing, making it look like AIRO."

"Very good, Matthews. Conclusion?"

I thought a minute. "Different shoes?"

"Exactamundo!"

"Which shoe was found where?" I asked.

"The one with the word intact was the one near where the car was pulled out of the lake."

"So where does that leave us?"

"The same place we were before, but with two mystery shoes instead of one."

"Great. What do we do now?"

He scratched his red head. "We go visit the two people who we know have shoes like these, then take it from there."

We stood on Mary Beth's front porch, waiting for someone to answer the doorbell. I was secretly hoping no one was home. No such luck.

The door opened and Judge Wainwright gave us a big smile. "Well, if it isn't the two best detectives in town. Come on in."

"Is Mary Beth home, Judge?" Clooz asked, his face a little redder than usual from the compliment.

"No, she ran down to the store for a minute. She'll be back soon if you'd like to wait."

"Sure," Clooz said.

Judge Wainwright started to lead us to the kitchen when Clooz spoke up.

"Judge, would it be all right if we waited in Mary Beth's room? There's something I would like to try on her computer."

"Sure, Clooz, help yourself. I'll send her up when she gets home."

"Great. Thanks."

We made our way up the stairs to Mary Beth's room.

"Why did you want to wait up here, Clooz? I bet Mrs. Wainwright would have given us some pie or something if we'd waited in the kitchen."

"Matthews, the case is much more important than your need for food. This is our opportunity to search Mary Beth's room without her around to ask a bunch of questions."

Of course, he was right, again. But Mrs. Wainwright's pie sure is good!

Clooz went over and switched on Mary Beth's computer in case the judge came up to check on us. Then he opened the closet. On a hanger in the back was a dark-blue Dallas Cowboys hooded sweatshirt.

And right there on the floor of the closet lay a pair of muddy AEROs.

Clooz picked them up and examined the soles. They looked just like the impression with the word AERO intact.

"Gotcha," Clooz said.

"Got who?" Mary Beth said as she walked into the room.

Chapter 14

My heart almost stopped, and Clooz's face looked like it was going to catch fire.

"Uh, what?" Clooz said.

"You said, 'Gotcha,' and I said, 'Got who?'" Mary Beth said, clearly annoyed.

"I, uh, I said 'Got tuh,' you know, got tuh go to the bathroom. Is that okay?"

She and I both looked at him like he was nuts, but she finally said, "Sure, it's down the hall on the left." Boy, was this embarrassing.

When Clooz had slunk off down the hall, Mary Beth asked, "What are you guys up to?"

"Well, uh, we haven't seen you around lately, and, uh, we thought we'd drop by and see how you were doing. Clooz really misses you helping us on this case."

"He does?" she asked unbelievingly.

"You bet. He was just saying on the way over how he wished you could have been with us the other night when Amanda's car was stolen. He figures you might have helped catch the thief. By the way, where were you that night?"

"Why do you want to know?" she asked suspiciously.

I put on my best innocent face. "Just curious, that's all. We just about got eaten up by bugs, and we mentioned how you were probably sitting in front of the TV eating ice cream and taking it easy."

Boy I was digging myself in deep now.

"I went to a movie with Amanda and her friend Julie. Then we did go for ice cream, that is Julie and I did; Amanda wasn't feeling well and went home."

"Stay out late, did you?" I asked casually.

"Yeah, pretty late. The movie was one of those late-night previews that didn't get out until eleven-thirty."

I was about to question her more when Clooz came back.

"Well, Matthews, it's time for us to go. We're probably keeping Mary Beth from her homework or something."

"Uh, sure," I mumbled.

Mary Beth just stared at us silently as we left. I couldn't help but believe that she knew us well enough to know we had something up our sleeve.

"I can't believe you just left me there alone with Mary Beth while you made up an excuse to go to the bathroom."

He grinned. "You're just ticked because you didn't think of it first."

I had to admit he was right.

"What were you doing in there so long?" I asked.

He reached into his pocket and pulled out a plastic bag. "I was carefully picking these hairs out of her brush. What were you doing?"

"Mostly making excuses for you. I told Mary Beth how you missed her being in on the case, especially the stakeout at Amanda's the other night."

"You're kidding. And you said all that with a straight face?"

"It was hard, but I found out where she was when the car was stolen."

Clooz was obviously impressed. "Are you going to share it or keep it to yourself?"

I paused a second to give him the impression I was thinking of keeping the information, but when he started to look impatient, I gave it up.

"She went to a movie with Julie."

"Who's Julie?"

"Amanda's friend."

"So, what's so special about that?"

I grinned. "Amanda went with them."

He screwed his face into a question mark. "So?"

"Amanda left just before midnight to go home because she was sick."

"She told us she spent the night with a friend," Clooz guessed.

"Exactamundo," I said triumphantly.

Chapter 15

We walked toward Amanda's house and discussed the case. There were some things that bugged me.

"You know, I was thinking. What if it turns out that Amanda really did spend the night with a friend?"

"It means that, with Mary Beth's alibi, Johnny looks more guilty."

"Okay, I'm with you there, but what if Amanda didn't spend the night with a friend? I can't really see how it'd matter, I mean, there's no way she stole her own car, right?"

"I agree, Matthews. That particular theory makes absolutely no sense."

"So, we're right back where we started, huh?"

He frowned thoughtfully, his blue eye squinting while his brown eye stayed wide open. "That's true unless Amanda doesn't back up Mary Beth's alibi. Then we've got more investigating to do."

Oh, boy, just what *I* wanted.

It was now our duty to check out Amanda's story, so we figured we'd get right on it. Amanda answered the door herself.

"Clooz, Matthews, what brings you here?"

"Nothing much," Clooz said, "just a few questions to clear up."

"Sure," she said. "Let's go up to my room where we can talk."

Clooz sat at Amanda's desk, and she plopped down on the bed. There was really nowhere else to sit, so I remained standing.

"What do you want to know?" she asked cautiously. Her guard was up for sure.

Clooz put on his serious detective face. "Amanda, there are just a few areas we have to clear up about your car."

"I thought you guys would be working on something else since you solved the haunting problem."

"We just want to tie up some loose ends to help out the police," I said.

Clooz gave me a look that said he was amazed at my quick reply. Hey, I'm not just a pretty face, you know. I've got a brain. It's just that, with Clooz's brain around, mine doesn't get much practice.

"Uh, okay, what do you want to know?"

Her hands were wrestling each other in her lap, and she was fidgeting a lot.

"Where were you when your car was stolen?"

"I told you, I spent the night with a friend."

"Uh-huh. Did you go anywhere else, like before you went to your friend's?"

She stared silently, like she was thinking, then she brightened. "Oh, you must mean the movie! I went to the movie with Julie and Mary Beth."

"I see. Why didn't you tell us that before?"

"Well, uh, I thought you meant where was I at the exact time the car was stolen." She smiled in satisfaction with her answer.

"So you spent the night with Julie?"

She nodded.

"And you and Mary Beth went to Julie's right after the movie?"

This was getting too tense for me, so I figured I'd use a trick I had just recently learned.

"Uh, excuse me, Amanda. Where's the bathroom?"

She pointed down the hall, and I shot Clooz a cute little smile as I hotfooted it out of there. I closed the bathroom door. I spotted a drinking glass, put it against the wall, and listened. I could hear their voices coming through.

"We went to get ice cream afterward."

"All of you?"

"Well, no, Mary Beth said she wasn't feeling well and went home."

"And what time was this?"

"Just before midnight, probably eleven-thirty."

That was all I needed to hear. I began looking for Amanda's hairbrush. I pulled open a drawer and there it was. I didn't have a bag to put it in (I was sure Clooz would bust me for not being prepared), so I plucked a tissue out of the dispenser and wrapped several strands in that.

I was feeling pretty pleased with myself now, so I decided to investigate further. I stuck the glass back up to the wall just to make sure they were still talking, then proceeded to search the bathroom. I opened the closet and guess what I found? That's right. A nice muddy pair of Aeros. And, oh, yes, the E in the word AERO had the horizontal legs plugged up with hardened gunk.

Chapter 16

Clooz looked relieved when I came back from the bathroom. He quickly told Amanda we had all the info we needed, thanked her for her time, and we left.

"Sounds like we have conflicting stories," I said as we hoofed it down the street toward the treehouse.

"It certainly seems so," he said thoughtfully. Then he asked, "Find anything in the bathroom?"

I grinned. "Oh, yeah. There's a pair of muddy Aeros in the closet with the E messed up just like the footprint we found."

"Great!"

"Well, kinda."

"What do you mean, kinda?" Clooz asked.

"It means the footprint close to where the car was found was Mary Beth's."

"Yeah, you're right, Matthews. It doesn't look good for her, does it?"

I shrugged. "I got some hair out of Amanda's brush, if it matters. Did you find anything out after I left?"

"Uh-huh. She said Mary Beth was sick and went home before they went for ice cream."

"I heard that part."

"How in the heck did you hear that? That was after you went to the bathroom."

"The old glass-to-the-wall trick," I said proudly.

"Heck, Matthews, I'm going to make a detective out of you yet!"

"Maybe," I said, puffing my chest out a little. Then I asked, "Anything else?"

"Just one more piece to the puzzle," he said. "There's a dark-blue Cowboys sweatshirt hanging in her closet."

"Wow, that seems like too much of a coincidence."

"Uh-huh. And I don't believe in coincidences in detective work."

We thought about that a minute, then I asked, "What now?"

"Well, to make the investigation complete, I guess we need to check out Johnny's house for clues, then see where we go from there."

Sounded like a plan to me. Not a good plan, as it turned out, but a plan nonetheless.

It was starting to get dark when we got to the 6C's clubhouse. No lights were on and the place looked deserted. That was the good news. The bad news was that you could only get in through the new shop, which was closed, or through the back fence, where the dogs were. But as usual, Clooz found an alternative.

We were standing under a high window at the side of the clubhouse. There was just enough room to stand between the building and a tall fence that separated the Chavez property from the lot next door.

"Where do you think that window goes, Matthews?"

"Probably to the bathroom."

"Well, we've been spending a lot of time in bathrooms lately, so I guess we'll feel right at home," Clooz said, his teeth glowing as he grinned at me in the dark.

It wasn't funny, but I laughed nervously.

"Want to give me a boost?"

I bent over and cupped my hands and Clooz put his foot in them, steadying himself with a hand on my shoulder. I heard a scraping sound that indicated the window had opened. Oh, lucky me.

I boosted Clooz up through the window and saw the beam from his pocket flashlight dart around the inside.

"See anything?" I whispered.

"Yuck," I heard him say, his voice sounding disgusted.

"What's wrong?"

"It's a bathroom all right, and I found out the hard way," he grumbled.

"How's that?"

"I stepped in the toilet, if you must know."

"Gross," I giggled.

"Hardy, har, har," he said from inside. "Very funny. Now get in here."

I was afraid he'd say that. I grabbed hold of the windowsill and pulled myself up. I guess those chin-ups in gym class were good for something.

I managed to get my arms through the window and drag my body behind. I scrunched through the opening and dropped to the floor, being careful to avoid the open toilet. Clooz could have closed the lid to make sure I didn't befall the same fate as he, but noooo . . .

I saw his light bouncing around the adjoining room and went to check it out. It looked the same as last time, just a little messier. He walked around, flashing his light in every nook and cranny, his wet sneaker squooshing with every step he took.

I saw him open the closet door and then mumble, "Ah, ha!"

"Find something!" I asked.

"Dark-blue Cowboys sweatshirt."

"Sounds incriminating."

"It does at that, Matthews. Why don't you get a hair sample from Johnny's comb in the bathroom, and I'll finish up here."

I walked into the bathroom and flipped on the light. Johnny's comb was in a drawer under the sink and luckily it had a few hairs in it. Remembering how greasy his hair was the last time I saw him, I used a tissue to remove the hair and wrapped it up and stuck it in my pocket, taking care to put it in a different pocket from the one that held Amanda's hair. I flipped off the light.

I could still hear Clooz squishing around in Johnny's room and whispered, "You ready yet?"

"Just about," came the reply.

I stood in the bathroom, waiting, listening to the cars pass by on the street outside. That was when I heard a car door slam.

"Clooz!" I whispered as loud as I dared. "A car!"

No reply.

In a few seconds I heard the back door open, followed by the click, click, click of toenails on the concrete floor. The dogs!

Trembling there in the dark, I tried to picture the bathroom in my head. Where could I hide? No place but the tub. I stepped in and pulled the shower curtain closed. I could hear the dogs sniffing around the other room, and Johnny talking to them, even though I couldn't make out what he was saying.

Then one of the dogs growled. Then the other started in. Then there was a bark. A growl. Another bark.

Then I heard Clooz say, "Hey, leave me alone!"

"What are you doing here, you little creep?" Johnny yelled.

I couldn't hear Clooz's reply.

"Where's that black kid you hang out with?"

No answer.

"Jake, Mack! Search, boys!"

The boys went into a frenzy. There were all kinds of yelping and sniffing and growling noises. I knew I was dead meat, but all I could do was stay in the tub. If I stepped out to surrender, the dogs would have me for dinner.

It only took a few seconds. I heard growling. Close. Then sniffing. Closer. Then one of the dogs started barking like crazy. The shower curtain puffed inward with every bark.

Then the curtain flew back and there stood Johnny Starke.

Chapter 17

Johnny marched me into the room where Clooz was sitting on the bed, looking disgusted. Starke motioned for me to join him.

The dogs took positions on each side of Starke like bookends as he stood in front of us, anger painting deep red lines across his face.

"Okay, I warned you kids about messing with me. Now you're going to have to pay."

He picked up the phone and punched a number. All he said was, "Bring the guys. I caught the snoops again."

That didn't sound too good for us.

Johnny sneered at us. "My buds will be here in a minute, and we'll pack you guys off to the lake. Believe me, they won't find you like they did Amanda's car."

"Then you *are* the one who stole it?" I asked bravely.

He shook his head. "No way, man. I'm not a thief, even though I know you little creeps were in here trying to find some evidence so you can pin it on me."

"Actually, it was just the opposite," Clooz said.

"Huh?"

Clooz explained. "Tony hired us to prove you didn't steal Amanda's car. We have been working on the case and have found a few things."

"So you know I didn't do it?"

"We're not convinced just yet. There are several pieces of evidence that don't look good for you, but there are other things that say you might not have done it."

"So," I continued, "if you'll just let us go, we'll finish our investigation and maybe get you off the hook."

He almost went for it. I could see him thinking it over. Then he quickly shook his head from side to side, his greasy hair swinging like wet rope.

"Uh-uh. The cops think I did it, and even if you told them I didn't, they wouldn't believe a couple of kids."

I was about to argue further when his friends, or buds, as he called them, walked in. I recognized them from the time before. It looked like they might be able to actually hurt us this time.

"Let's get them out of here before Chavez can rescue them," the one with the bad breath said.

The others agreed, and the two newcomers grabbed us and pushed us toward the door. I struggled against them, but when the dogs started growling, I relaxed. No use getting eaten alive here. I'd wait until I had a better chance later—if I lived that long.

The guy with the bad breath reached for the door, but it suddenly exploded inward and almost knocked him down.

"Freeze!" Detective Merkin yelled, pointing his pistol directly at Stinky Breath.

Boy, was I glad to see him!

Chapter 18

At least I was glad until I heard Sergeant Steele's booming voice precede him through the door. When he appeared, his jaws were clamped tightly around his cigar, and his face was as red as a stop sign.

Mary Beth followed him in.

"I said, what's going on here?"

"You guys okay?" Mary Beth interrupted.

"Fine," we both said together.

Oh boy, the sarge was hot now.

"Merkin," he yelled, "load these kids up and take them to the station. We'll get some answers there."

Merkin was kind of frozen, his gun still pointed at Stinky Breath, not looking like he wanted to do as he was ordered.

Clooz saved him the trouble.

"Sergeant Steele, we were hired by Tony Chavez to prove that Johnny didn't steal Amanda's car. Johnny came in and saw us here and called for his buddies to help get rid of us. Then you came. That's it."

"That's it? *That's it?* I can't believe you're trying to tell me that's it."

"What do you mean, Sergeant?" Clooz asked innocently.

"Well, for starters, you probably broke in here. That's breaking and entering, as well as trespassing. That's enough to run you in, right there. I'm sure Starke here would want to press charges."

Johnny was nodding vigorously.

"I know it doesn't look good, Sergeant, but I think I can solve this whole mess if you'll just let me make two phone calls. If you or Johnny still want me arrested, I'll go quietly, without another word."

Steele stared silently for a minute, then nodded. It was too good a deal to pass up. "This I got to see."

Clooz took Johnny's phone into the bathroom to make the calls.

While we were waiting, I asked Mary Beth, "Did you call the cops?"

"Yep, I've been following you ever since you left my house. When you went to Amanda's and then here, I knew something was up. Then I saw Johnny come home, and I knew you were in trouble, so I ran to the nearest house to use the phone. There was no one home, so I tried another. No luck. Finally, someone was home at the third house but wouldn't let me use the phone. I called from the fourth house, all the way in the next block."

"I'm glad you did."

She smiled.

Clooz came out of the bathroom and told us that Amanda was on her way over.

We waited mostly in silence. Johnny and his two buddies kind of sulked and looked nervous the whole time. Made me think there might be something there they didn't want the cops to see.

Steele quietly chewed on his cigar, a slight grin on his face, figuring he was finally going to get to bust Clooz Calahan. I knew better.

There was a knock on the door and Merkin let Amanda in.

"What's going on here?" she asked when she saw all the people.

"Clooz is going to tell us who stole your car," I said.

"Yeah, right," Sergeant Steele snickered.

Clooz ignored him and took the floor.

"First of all, let me review what we know about the perpetrator."

Stinky Breath said, "The what?"

"The one who committed the crime, lame brain," Mary Beth said.

Clooz continued. "The suspect wore white sneakers and a dark-blue sweatshirt with a hood. That's all we knew. Then, we investigated the scene of the crime. There we found one piece of evidence."

"I didn't hear about any evidence," Sergeant Steele bellowed at Clooz.

Clooz held up his hand. "Please allow me to finish, Sergeant."

Steele grumbled, but kept quiet.

"What was the evidence?" Merkin asked.

"A ballpoint pen."

"So?" Mary Beth said.

"It was from Chavez Auto Repair."

Everyone immediately looked at Johnny. Mary Beth looked surprised. Steele leaned forward to hear better.

"And it had fingerprints on it."

"Whose?" they all asked together.

"Johnny's and . . ." he paused.

"Who else's?" Mary Beth asked.

Clooz took a deep breath. "Yours, Mary Beth."

Chapter 19

Mary Beth shot up like a rocket.

"I can explain . . ."

Clooz cut her off. "Please, everyone, you'll have time to defend yourselves later. Let me continue."

Mary Beth sat back down, fuming. I think I saw a puff of smoke come out of her right ear.

"Then," Clooz continued, "when the car was recovered, we investigated the scene and found more evidence." He hesitated, but no one said a word. He had them now.

"We found two sets of footprints and a blond hair."

Everyone looked at Mary Beth. She didn't say anything, but her face got a shade redder.

"Through our investigation, we found out who the shoes belonged to: Mary Beth and Amanda."

Everyone looked at Amanda with surprise, but they all kept quiet. Now Amanda's face was red, too.

"Then, we began to check everyone's alibi. We all know Johnny didn't have one, but Mary Beth and Amanda went to the movies together with Amanda's friend Julie. And then they went for ice cream. This was about thirty minutes before Matthews and I saw someone steal the car.

"There was a problem, though. Mary Beth said Amanda didn't go with them for ice cream. She said Amanda got sick and went home. But when we asked Amanda about it, she said Mary Beth was the one who got sick. So the question became, who went with Julie to get ice cream?"

Amanda's face was scarlet and she was squirming.

"Amanda," Clooz said. "Do you want to tell us who went for ice cream?"

"I . . . I did, of course."

"She's lying!" Mary Beth exclaimed. "I went with Julie for ice cream."

Clooz looked at Mary Beth and said, "I know."

A hush fell over the room while everyone looked at Amanda.

"What are you all looking at me for? I didn't steal my own car, for goodness sake! I don't even have a Cowboys sweatshirt!"

Clooz smiled really big. "As a matter of fact,

Amanda, you do. I saw it in your closet when I was at your house today. Besides, I never said it was a Cowboys sweatshirt the thief was wearing, only that it was dark blue. How else would you have known if you weren't the thief?"

Everyone began talking at once, but even over all of that noise, I could hear Amanda crying.

Chapter 20

Johnny walked over to Amanda. "Why did you do it, Amanda? I mean, I really liked you and you almost got me sent to jail."

Amanda could do nothing but sob.

"Perhaps I can answer that," Clooz said. "Amanda was really mad at you because you haunted her car, but, more importantly, because she thought you were the one who would keep her out of the 6C's.

"She figured that if you went off to jail, then you wouldn't be a threat anymore."

"But why did she make it look like I did it?" Mary Beth asked.

Clooz smiled. "She was just lucky there. When you threatened Johnny, she figured she could steal the car, and even if Johnny wasn't convicted, the blame would then be diverted to you. She figured no one would suspect her of stealing her own car."

"But why did she trash her car?" I asked. "Why not just hide it?"

He nodded toward the garage, where the car had been. "If you really look at the car closely, you'll see that it's only dirty with four flat tires. Amanda was very careful not to drive it into the lake too far."

Sergeant Steele and Detective Merkin had been silent all this time. I think they were a little sad about the way things worked out. I know I was. Steele walked over and gently touched Amanda's arm.

"You better come with me, Amanda. After I read you your rights, we'll go to the police station and you can call your parents."

As Amanda was being led out of the room in handcuffs, Johnny stepped in front of her. "Did you really hate me that much?"

She looked at him sadly and nodded.

"Wow," he said, shaking his head. "It looks like I've got a lot to learn about being a friend."

Amanda smiled. "Yeah, me too."

Sergeant Steele led her through the door. Then he stuck his head back in and said, "Don't think you're off the hook for this, Calahan. We've got some talking to do about withholding evidence."

Detective Merkin winked at Clooz as they left.

A week later we were sitting at the monthly meeting of the 6C's. Tony was at the front of the room.

"I'd like to nominate some kids for honorary members of the 6C's. First, there's Clooz Calahan, who stuck by us until he found the real car thief. Do I hear a second?"

Johnny Starke was the first one to stand. "I'll second the nomination."

Clooz was grinning from ear to ear.

"All in favor?"

Everyone stood and yelled, "Aye!"

Tony continued. "And then there's Matthews, who risked his life and limb to help Clooz solve the case. Second?"

A guy in the back of the room seconded the motion.

"All in favor?"

Once again, everyone yelled "Aye!"

"Great!" Tony said.

"Tony, I'd like to nominate another new member."

It was Johnny.

"Sure, Johnny," Tony said. "Who?"

Johnny smiled broadly and said, "I'd like to nominate the first female member of the 6C's, Mary Beth Wainwright!"

There was a whole chorus of seconds.

Mary Beth looked like she was about to float away on a cloud.

"All in favor?"

"Aye!" everyone said together, and a stirring round of applause broke out.

After the meeting, as the three of us were walking home, I said, "You know, Clooz, there's one thing that still bothers me."

"Only *one* thing bothers you?" Mary Beth wise-cracked as she looked at me.

I tried to stare her down, but finally broke out in a grin. "I mean about the case."

"What's that, Matthews?"

"Well, we found the hair at the lake, then we gathered hair samples from all the suspects, but we never did anything with the evidence. What was that all about?"

"You got some of my hair? When? How?" Mary Beth demanded.

"When we were at your house and I went to the bathroom. I got it out of your hairbrush," Clooz said.

"And you didn't even have a search warrant!" she grinned at him.

"Anyway . . ." I said, trying to get back on track.

"The hair was really useless," Clooz said. "I mean, the only way to really tell who it belonged to was through DNA testing, and the cops would never have done that just for a car theft."

"Then why?"

"Well, the hair was very long. Longer than Johnny's or yours, Mary Beth. So I figured I might need to use it to trick Amanda into confessing."

"Okay, I'll buy that, but how did the hair get that high up in the tree? And why was Amanda's footprint under the tree and not by where the car was ditched? And while we're talking about the car, why was Mary Beth's footprint by the car, and how did her fingerprints get on the pen we found in Amanda's garage?"

"I thought you said only *one* thing was bugging you about the case," Mary Beth said.

"Okay, so I underestimated my ignorance."

"First time that's happened, I bet," Mary Beth said.

"Okay, you two, do you want the answers or do you want to argue?"

We shut up and listened.

"Let's start with the pen. You want to tell him, Mary Beth?"

She took a deep breath. "Amanda and I were looking at her car and I found the pen on the floor. I picked it up and put it on the dashboard. It must have rolled off and fallen out of the car later."

"That sounds reasonable," I said. "What about the footprints?"

"Mary Beth can verify this, but I suspect she was snooping around the crime scene before the cops got there." He looked at her for confirmation.

She nodded. "I was listening to my dad's scanner and heard about the car being found. I hopped on my bike and rode out there. I didn't even think about leaving footprints," she said, slightly embarrassed.

"Okay, then how do you explain there not being any of Amanda's footprints where the car was found?"

He grinned his I'm-a-great-detective grin and said, "When Amanda parked the car, she simply climbed out and walked across the back of the car to avoid stepping in the water. She didn't even open the door. Remember the car was found with the top down."

Darn. He got me again. I decided to give it one more shot. "How do you explain how the hair got up in that tree?"

He gave us the grin again. "Elementary, my dear Matthews. When Amanda climbed out of the driver's seat and stood up, she bumped her head on the branch of the tree overhead."

As usual, Clooz had all the bases covered. "So you mean, if you'd had to use the hair as evidence to get her to confess, she would have been . . ."

"Guilty by a hair!" we all said at once.